Anonymous

Fourth Annual Report of the Superintendent of the Public School of the City of Chicago, for the Year Ending February 1, 1858

SALZWASSER
VERLAG

Anonymous

Fourth Annual Report of the Superintendent of the Public School of the City of Chicago, for the Year Ending February 1, 1858

Reprint of the original.

1st Edition 2023 | ISBN: 978-3-37514-334-3

Verlag (Publisher): Salzwasser Verlag GmbH, Zeilweg 44, 60439 Frankfurt, Deutschland
Vertretungsberechtigt (Authorized to represent): E. Roepke, Zeilweg 44, 60439 Frankfurt, Deutschland
Druck (Print): Books on Demand GmbH, In de Tarpen 42, 22848 Norderstedt, Deutschland

FOURTH

ANNUAL REPORT

OF THE

SUPERINTENDENT

OF THE

PUBLIC SCHOOL

OF THE

CITY OF CHICAGO,

FOR THE

Year Ending February 1, 185૬

CHICAGO:

CHICAGO DAILY PRESS, BOOK AND JOB PRINT, 45 CLARK STR

1858.

CITY OF CHICAGO.

At a meeting of the Board of Education, March 20, 1858 :

Ordered, That six thousand copies of the Annual Report of the Superintendent of Public Schools be printed for distribution.

Attest :

W. H. WELLS, *Secretary.*

REPORT.

To the Board of Education of the City of Chicago :

GENTLEMEN : In my last Report, I referred at
length to the children that are growing up in our
midst without the benefits of school instruction, and
presented a detailed account of the organization of
the High School.

HISTORICAL SKETCH.

I propose to introduce the present Report with a
brief historical sketch of the public school system of
the city.

It will be necessary to allude first to the means of
education that were enjoyed before the public schools
were established.

The first regular tuition given in Chicago was in
the winter of 1810–11, by Robert A. Forsyth, late
Paymaster in the United States Army ; and the first
pupil was our present respected citizen, John H.
Kinzie, Esq. The teacher was about thirteen years
of age, and the pupil six.

The principal aid employed in this course of

private lessons was a spelling-book, that had been brought from Detroit to Chicago in a chest of tea. The first school taught in Chicago was opened in the fall of 1816, by William L. Cox, a discharged soldier, in a log building, belonging to John Kinzie, Esq. The house had been occupied as a bakery, and stood in the back part of Mr. Kinzie's garden, near the present crossing of Pine and Michigan streets, just east of the Lake House. The children composing this school were John H. Kinzie, with two of his sisters and one brother, and three or four children from the Fort.

There was a small school in the Garrison, taught by a sergeant, about 1820.

In 1829, Charles H. Beaubien, son of J. B. Beaubien, Esq., Agent of the American Fur Company, taught a small family school, near the Garrison, embracing the children of Messrs. J. B. and Mark Beaubien.

In June, 1830, Mr. Stephen Forbes commenced a school near the place now marked by the meeting of Randolph street and Michigan Avenue. This was on the west bank of the Chicago river, which then flowed in a southerly direction and emptied near the foot of Madison street. He was employed by J. B. Beaubien, Esq., and Lieut. Hunter. The school numbered about twenty-five pupils, from four years of age to twenty, and embraced the children of Mr. J. B. Beaubien, those belonging to the Fort, and a few others. It was taught in a large, low, gloomy log building, containing five rooms. The walls of the school room were afterwards enlivened by a tapestry of white cotton sheeting. The house belonged to

Mr. Beaubien, and had been previously occupied by the sutler of the Fort. Mr. Forbes resided in the same building, and was assisted in school by Mrs. Forbes. After continuing the school about one year, he was succeeded by Mr. Foot. Mr. Forbes was afterward Sheriff of Cook county. His present residence is Newburg, Ohio.

In October, 1831, Richard I. Hamilton, Esq., was appointed Commissioner of School Lands for Cook county, and the School Fund remained in his charge till 1840.

In spring of 1833, Col. Hamilton and Col. Owen employed Mr. John Watkins to instruct a small school in the North Division, near the old Indian Agency House, in which Col. Hamilton then resided. Its location would now be marked by the crossing of Wolcott and North Water streets. The same two gentlemen afterwards built a house, in which Mr. Watkins continued his school, on the north bank of the river, just east of Clark street. This was the first house built for a school in Chicago.

In the Autumn of 1833, Miss Eliza Chappel, now the wife of Rev. Jeremiah Porter, of Green Bay, opened an Infant School, of about twenty children, in a log house, on South Water street, a short distance west of the grounds belonging to the Fort. A portion of the children attending this school were from the families connected with the Garrison.

In the latter part of the same year, 1833, Mr. G. T. Sproat came from Boston and opened an English and Classical School for Boys, in a small house of worship belonging to the First Baptist Church, on South Water street, near Franklin.

In March, 1834, Miss Sarah L. Warren, now Mrs. Abel E. Carpenter, of Warrenville, was engaged as an assistant in Mr. Sproat's school.* The school section of the original township is situated near the centre of the city. In October, 1833, all but four of the one hundred and forty-two blocks of this section were sold at auction for $38,865, on a credit of one, two and three years.† The remaining four blocks are now valued at about $700,000. The value of that portion which was sold is now estimated at about $12,000,000.

The Infant School of Miss Chappel met with

---

* The following extract from one of Mrs. Carpenter's letters will give some idea of the surroundings of the schools at that period:

"I boarded at Elder Freeman's. His house must have been situated some four or five blocks southeast of the school, near Mr. Snow's, with scarce a house between. What few buildings there were then were mostly on Water street. I used to go across without regard to streets. It was not uncommon, in going to and from school, to see *prairie wolves*, and we could hear them howl any time in the day. We were frequently annoyed by *Indians;* but the great difficulty we had to encounter was *mud.* No person now can have a just idea of what Chicago mud used to be. Rubbers were of no account. I purchased a pair of gentlemen's brogans, and fastened them tight about the ancle, but would still go over them in mud and water, and was obliged to have a pair of men's boots made."

† The following is a copy of the Petition for the sale of the school lands:

"*To the Commissioner of School Lands for the County of Cook, in the State of Illinois:*

"The undersigned, your petitioners, inhabitants of Congressional Township thirty-nine north, range fourteen east, represent that they are desirous of having section number sixteen in said township sold for the purpose for which it was given; and your petitioners are of opinion that it would promote their interest by selling said section on a credit of one, two and three years, under the provisions of the act authorizing a credit on sales of school lands, and at an interest of not less than ten per centum per annum, payable semi-annually in advance."

This petition received ninety-five signatures, embracing most of the principal citizens of the town.

general favor in the town, and in the Summer of 1834 it was removed, for better accommodations, to the First Presbyterian Church. Though called an Infant School, and composed mostly of young children, a portion of the scholars were ten or twelve years of age.

By the School Law of 1833, the county commis- \ sioner was required to apportion the interest derived from each Township School Fund among the several teachers in the town, according to the number of their scholars residing in the township, and the number of days each scholar was instructed; on condition, however, that the Trustees of the several schools should first present a certificate that the teachers had given gratuitous instruction to all such orphans and children of indigent parents residing in the vicinity, as had been presented for that purpose.

In 1834 an appropriation was made to Miss Chappel from the School Fund of the town, and the school taught by her at that time, in the First Presbyterian Church, on the west side of Clark street, between Lake and Randolph, was properly the *first public school of Chicago.*

Miss Chappel's school at length became a boarding school for older pupils, and a considerable number came from other townships and boarded with her and her assistants. One object of the school at this time, was to train up teachers for the common schools in the new settlements. The Infant Deprtment was still continued, and both branches of the school occupied the same room in the church, being separated by a curtain.

In the Winter of 1834–5, Miss Chappel resigned

her charge,* and the school passed into the hands of Miss Ruth Leavenworth, afterwards Mrs. Joseph Hanson.

This school received much sympathy and aid from John S. Wright, Esq., who built a house for its use at his own expense. This house was situated on the west side of Clark street, just south of Lake. It was first occupied by Miss Leavenworth's school.

The school taught in the Baptist Church, on Water street, became a public school in 1834.† During this year Mr. Sproat was succeeded by Henry Van Der- bogart, M. D., who also resigned before the close of the year, and was succeeded by Mr. Thomas Wright. In 1835, the school was committed to the care of Mr. James McClellen. Miss Warren was engaged as an assistant in this school from March, 1834, to June, 1836.

In the Winter of 1834–5, Mr. George Davis had a school over a store, on Lake street, between Dearborn and Clark. In 1835, Mr. Davis taught a public school in the Presbyterian Church on Clark street; and the school of Mr. Watkins, which had now become a public school, was also continued on the North side of the river.

In February, 1835, an act was passed by the Legis- lature of the State, in relation to Schools, in Town-

---

* Mrs. Porter's passion for teaching is so strong and abiding, that after the lapse of a quarter of a century, she has returned to her former employment, and is at the present time engaged as a teacher in one of the Primary Schools at Green Bay.

† I regret that I am not able to speak more definitely of the distinction between public and private schools at this period. The books which were kept by Col. Hamilton from 1833 to 1837, and which passed into the hands of is successor, I have not been able to find.

ship Thirty-nine North, and Range Fourteen East, which contained the following provisions:

1. The legal voters of the town were to elect annually, on the first Monday in June, "either five or seven persons to be School Inspectors."

2. The Inspectors were to recommend to the County Commissioners to lay off and divide the Township into school districts; and the Commissioners were required to lay off, divide, and alter the districts, as the School Inspectors might from time to time recommend.

3. The Inspectors were to examine teachers, visit the schools, prescribe text-books, etc.

4. "The legal voters in each school district, shall annually elect three persons to be Trustees of Common Schools, whose duty it shall be to employ qualified and suitable teachers; to see that the schools are *free*, and that all white children in the district have an opportunity of attending them, under such regulations as the Inspectors may make; to take charge of the school houses, and all of the school property belonging to the district, and to manage the whole financial concerns thereof. The said Trustees shall annually levy and collect a tax sufficient to defray the necessary expense of fuel, rent of school room, and furniture for the same; and they shall levy and collect such additional taxes as a majority of the legal voters of the district, at a meeting called for that purpose, shall direct: *Provided*, That such additional taxes shall never exceed one-half of one per cent. per annum upon all the taxable property in the district; all of which taxes the said Trustees shall have full power to assess and collect."

In November, 1835, the town was divided into four School Districts. District No. 1, was in the North Division of the city, and the designation of the other districts was entirely different from that which has since been adopted. The whole number of schools in the town at that time, including both public and private schools, was seven.

In the Spring of 1836, Miss Leavenworth's school, which had been taught in Mr. Wright's building, was discontinued, and Miss Frances L. Willard opened in the same place a school for the instruction of young ladies in the higher branches of education. Miss Louisa Gifford, now Mrs. Dr. Dyer, was afterwards employed as an assistant, and a Primary Department was opened.

In the Spring of 1837, this school, which had now become a public school, passed into the hands of Miss Gifford, and Miss Willard opened another school of a similar character.

In 1836, and till March, 1837, Mr. John Brown taught a private school in the North Division, near the corner of Dearborn and Wolcott streets.

In March, 1837, Mr. Edward Murphy opened a private school in the same building. This building was afterwards rented by the Trustees of the District, and Mr. Murphy was employed to teach a public school from August, 1837, to November, 1838.* His salary was $800 per annum. Mr. Murphy now resides at Evanston.

Mr. McClellen, who took charge of the school in the Baptist Church, on Water street, in 1835, continued to teach a public school till 1838.

In March, 1837, Chicago became a city. By the

---

* In answer to my inquiries respecting this school, Mr. Murphy has kindly furnished the following incident, which explains the mode in which he first established his authority in school:

"My predecessor was Mr. J. B., of whom I rented the school room, during his unexpired lease of the premises. Some of Mr. B.'s pupils had beat him severely, in consequence of which he resigned.

"An incident, connected with the opening of my school, may not be out of place. I addressed the pupils, some thirty-six in number, pointed out the necessity of strictly observing the rules by which the school should be governed, and that a departure from the strict observance of the rules would subject any pupil to a merited chastisement.

"The day after, I placed an oak sapling, an inch in diameter, on my desk. That afternoon, a Mr. S., who owned the building, came into the school room; and seeing the walls decorated with caricatures, and the likeness of almost every animal, from a rabbit to an elephant, got in a raging passion, and used rather abusive language. I complained; he became more violent; I walked to my desk, took the sapling, and shouted, *clear out*, which he obeyed by a rapid movement. This trifling incident effectually calmed the ringleaders, some of whom now occupy honorable and respectable positions in society."

conditions of the charter, the Common Council were made Commissioners of Schools for the city. They were to appoint, annually, not less than five nor more than twelve School Inspectors. The legal voters of each School District were to meet annually and elect three Trustees of Common Schools, as before.

The first Board of Inspectors, after the incorporation of the city, was elected May 12, 1837. It consisted of the following members:

THOMAS WRIGHT,   FRANCIS PEYTON,
N. H. BOLLES,   G. W. CHADWICK;
JOHN GAGE,   B. HUNTOON,
T. R. HUBBARD,   R. J. HAMILTON,
I. T. HINTON,   W. H. BROWN.

The teachers in the public school in 1837, beside those already named, were Miss Sarah Kellogg, and Messrs. A. Steel Hopkins, George C. Collins, Hiram Baker, C. S. Bailey, and Samuel C. Bennett. The school of Miss Kellogg, and those of Messrs. Collins and Bennett, were in the South Division; that of Mr. Bailey was in the West Division.

In 1838, public schools were taught by Messrs. McClellen, Murphy, Bennett, Collins, Bailey, Calvin De Wolf, and Thomas Hoyne. Mr. De Wolf succeeded Mr. Bailey, in the West Division.

In 1839, the School Fund was mostly unproductive, and the schools were in a depressed condition.

In 1839, a special act was passed by the Legislature, in relation to the Common Schools of Chicago, which laid the foundation of our present school system. By this act, the School Fund of Chicago was transferred from the charge of the School Commissioner of the county, and placed entirely under the control of the Common Council of the City. The Council were also empowered to raise money by taxation for the support of schools, and for the purpose of supplying the inadequacy of the fund for the support of teachers.

It was made the duty of the Council to appoint seven School Inspectors for the City, and three Trustees for each school district.*

In February, 1840, William H. Brown, Esq., was appointed School Agent, and assumed the charge of the School Fund of the city. This office he continued to hold for a period of thirteen years, and during the first portion of this time, he declined receiving any compensation for his services. It is worthy of remark, that Mr. Brown did not make a single loan by which the School Fund suffered a loss.

The first Board of School Inspectors, under the new organization, was composed of William Jones, J. Young Scammon, Isaac N. Arnold, Nathan H. Bowels, John Gray, J. H. Scott, and Hiram Hugunin. The first meeting of this Board was held in November, 1840, and William Jones was elected Chairman.

It is at this date, that the written Records of the public schools commence.

In December, 1840, an ordinance in relation to the Public Schools was prepared by J. Young Scammon, of the Board of Inspectors, and adopted by the Common Council.

The only public school teachers employed at this

---

* For the form of this act in relation to schools, which are drawn up with more than ordinary care and discrimination, the city is indebted to the pen of J. Y. Scammon, Esq.

time, were A. G. Rumsey, and H. B. Perkins, in the South Division; A. D. Sturtevant, in the West Division; and A. C. Dunbar, in the North Division. The salary paid to each of these teachers was \$33.33 a month.

From the regulations adopted by the Board of Inspectors in April, 1841, it appears that the schools were kept five days and a half a week,. with "a recess of a few minutes" each half day; and the amount of vacation allowed in a year, was four weeks.

Instruction in Vocal Music was first introduced into the public schools in January, 1842. The first teacher employed was Mr. N. Gilbert. Instruction in this department appears for a time to have met with considerable opposition. In January, 1843, it was ordered by the Common Council, that the School Inspectors "dispense with the services of a Music Teacher as soon as it can be done consistently with the present contracts."

In March, 1847, a motion was made by a member of the Council, that the Committee on Schools inquire into the expediency of making Vocal Music one of the permanent branches taught in the common schools. Another member moved to amend, by adding Dancing. The amendment receiving only three votes, was lost; and in January, 1848, a music teacher was employed.

In 1844, the first public school house was erected, on Madison street, between Dearborn and State. This important measure was, in a great degree, accomplished by the well-directed efforts of Ira Miltimore, Esq., who was, at that time, a member of the Common Council. The house was regarded by a large portion of the citizens as a monument of folly; and the Mayor elected the following year recommended, in his inaugural address, that the Council should either sell the house or convert it into an Insane Asylum; and build one, two or more small houses, suited to the wants of the city. This building is now occupied by the Dearborn School.

In December, 1850, the Common Council passed an ordinance, making it the duty of the teachers of the public schools to meet on Saturdays, and hold a Teachers' Institute, under the direction of the School Inspectors; and by a rule of the Board of Inspectors, the teachers were required to meet on the first, second and third Saturdays in each month, and remain in session not less than two hours at each meeting.

In October, 1852, the Board voted that the meetings of the Institute should be held on the first and third Saturdays of each month, from 10 to 12 A. M.; and in 1856, the number of meetings was reduced to one in a month, commencing at 9 A. M., and continuing till 12, with a recess of fifteen minutes.

In January, 1841, the public schools were taught by four male teachers. In January, 1846, five years later, there were three male teachers and six female teachers; in January, 1851, four male teachers, and twenty female teachers; and at the present time, March, 1858, there are seventeen male teachers and sixty-two female teachers.

The teachers that have been longest engaged in the public schools are Mr. A. D. Sturtevant, sixteen years; and Mr. A. G. Wilder, fourteen years.

After the re-organization of the schools in 1840, various improvements were, from time to time, introduced, but the general system remained substantially the same till the office of Superintendent was created. The following is a copy of the ordinance prescribing the duties of this office :

Section 1. The Superintendent of Public Schools shall act under the advice and direction of the Board of Education, and shall have the superintendence of all the public schools, school houses, books and apparatus: *Provided, however,* That repairs and improvements to the school houses and estates, and the furnishing of fuel, water, and school furniture, may be done under the direction of the " City Superintendent." He shall devote himself exclusively to the duties of his office. He shall keep regular office hours, other than school hours, at a place to be provided for that purpose, which place shall be the general depository of books and papers belonging to the Board of Education, and at which the Board shall hold its meetings. He shall acquaint himself with whatever principles and facts may concern the interests of popular education, and with all matters pertaining in any way to the organization, discipline and instruction of Public Schools, to the end that all the children in this city, who are instructed at the Public Schools, may obtain the best education which these schools are able to impart.

Sec. 2. He shall visit all the schools as often as his duties will permit, and shall pay particular attention to the classification of the pupils in the several schools, and to the apportionment among the several classes of the prescribed studies. In passing daily from school to school, he shall endeavor to transfer improvements and to remedy defects.

Sec. 3. He shall attend all the meetings of the Board of Education, and act as Secretary thereof. He shall keep the Board of Education constantly informed of the condition of the Public Schools, and the changes required in the same. He shall keep a record of all his proceedings, at all times open to the Board of Education. A general report of the condition of the Public Schools shall be prepared by him at the close of each school year for publication. He shall, moreover, report to the Board of Education, from time to time, such by-laws and regulations for the government, discipline and management of the Public Schools as he may deem expedient, and the same may be adopted by the Board ; and shall also perform such other duties as the Board of Education shall from time to time direct.

Sec. 4. The Superintendent shall carefully observe the teaching and discipline of all the teachers employed in the Public Schools, and shall report to the Board whenever he shall find any teacher deficient or incompetent in the discharge of his or her duties.

Mr. John C. Dore entered upon the duties of this office in May, 1854, and immediately introduced a thorough system of classification and gradation in all the schools, which has been continued to the present time. Mr. Dore resigned his situation in March, 1856, and in June, 1856, the present incumbent was appointed.

In 1854, the office of Trustees of the several School Districts was abolished, and the employment of teachers and the charge of the school property passed into the hands of the Board of Inspectors.

The establishment of the Chicago High School, in 1856, and the building of two new Grammar School Houses, on an improved plan, the same year, mark an important era in the history of the public schools.

The provisions of the Revised City Charter, approved February, 1857, re-organized the Board of Education upon a new plan, the principal features of which are an increase in the number of members, and a change in the length of time for which they are appointed.

The Board now consists of fifteen members instead of seven, one-third of whom are elected each year, for a period of three years. By this arrangement, two-thirds of the Board must always consist of members having either one or two years' experience, thus securing steadiness and uniformity of action, which are indispensible to the permanent prosperity of the schools.

As the records of the Board for the last eighteen years are always accessible, I have made only a few brief allusions to this period. The sketch which I have presented of the earlier history of the schools embodies the result of extensive inquiries among those who were personally engaged in the schools, and those who were interested in their welfare. Nearly all the statements introduced have been verified by comparing the recollections of several different persons, and I trust they will in the main be found reliable. If any one is able to furnish additional information in regard to the early history of our schools, it will be thankfully received.

I have attempted only an outline sketch, but I trust it will aid in perpetuating the memory of at least a few of those who have labored to plant the pillars on which our present system of popular education rests.

When in the far distant future the philosophic historian shall write the history of our city; when the character and the acts of successive generations shall be weighed in the scales of impartial judgment; when material wealth shall be regarded in its true light, as a means to an end; when social enjoyment, and intellectual cultivation, and moral worth shall be rightly estimated, as essential elements of prosperity in every community—then will the wisdom of those who have laid the foundations of our public school system be held in grateful remembrance; then will the names of Scammon, and Brown, and Jones, and Miltimore, and Moseley and Foster, and their coadjutors be honored as among the truest and most worthy benefactors of Chicago.

SCHOOL ACCOMMODATIONS.

In passing to consider the present condition of the public schools, the first subject that demands attention is the provision which is made by the city for their accommodation.

2

During the year, 1857, two first-class school houses were erected and mostly furnished, at an expense of about $28,000 each. The two together are designed to accommodate about 1200 scholars, and this number may be increased to 1300, by placing seats and desks in the hall of each house, for the Principal's division. Two similar houses were built in 1856, making the accommodations for pupils greater at the present time than they were two years ago, by more than 2500 seats; and yet so rapid has been the increase of the scholars, that the houses are more crowded now than they were two years since. Indeed, the most difficult problem which the city has to solve in relation to the public schools, is to find how sufficient room can be provided for the scholars from the present resources of the School Tax Fund.

The schools are sufficiently popular with all classes in the community, and the two-mills tax is cheerfully paid for their support. If our schools did not increase in a greater ratio than those of New York or Boston, the appropriations now made to them would be fully adequate to their necessities; but the demand for room has been so great, that more than two-thirds of the school appropriations for the last two years have been swallowed up in permanent investments for buildings and grounds; and now, after having exhausted the resources of the school treasury, we find that the schools are still crowded almost to suffocation, and the cry for room is louder than ever before.

The Board of Education have already recommended to the Common Council—

1. To erect two new houses during the present year, of sufficient size to accommodate from 800 to

1,000 pupils each; one in the North Division and one in the South Division.

2. To erect a building on the grounds now occupied by the Scammon School, of sufficient size to accommodate 400 pupils.

3. To procure lots and remove the frame buildings that now stand on the premises of the Brown and Foster Schools.

If all these recommendations should be carried into effect, the school accommodations of Chicago would even then be more limited than those of any other city of equal size in all the Northern States of the Union. But, from the investigations which have been made since these resolutions of the Board were adopted, it appears doubtful whether the school appropriations for the current year will warrant so large an expenditure for new buildings.

What then is to be done? Our city ordinances require that free instruction shall be provided for *all* the children residing within the limits of the city, who are over the age of five years, and who desire to attend the public schools; and yet there has been no time during the last two years when the number attending the schools would not have been greatly increased if suitable provision could have been made to receive them.

It is obvious that each year is now made to bear more than its legitimate proportion of the expense of erecting new houses. The appropriate expenses of any one year are ascertained by making a fair estimate of the rent of all the school buildings and grounds, and adding this amount to the current expenses. In this view of the subject, it will be seen that we are not only building houses for our own use, but also, in part, for those who are to come after us. If the houses were all built by private individuals and rented to the city for the use of the schools, no one would think if charging any one year with more than its own expenses; and yet during the year 1857, the amount paid by the city for new houses, and other permanent investments, for the schools, would be sufficient to furnish perpetual rent for more than twice the number of children now in the schools, and with far better accommodations than we now enjoy. We are thus paying for our accommodations more than twice their actual value, in order that those who come after us may have them at less than half their real cost.   But it is safe to presume that the Chicago of 1868 will be quite as able to pay her own expenses as the Chicago of 1858 is to pay so large a portion of them in advance. · Permit me then to inquire whether it is not practicable, by issuing bonds or otherwise, to make .some provision for aiding the School Tax Fund, in the erection of new buildings, without doing any injustice to those who are to enjoy the benefit of the investment in years to come?

If this measure should not be found feasible, I trust the resources of the School Tax Fund, for the current year, will, at least, prove sufficient to erect one large building in the North Division, and one small one, to increase the accommodations of the Scammon School, beside purchasing grounds for the frame houses now standing on the premises of the Brown and Foster schools.

This would leave a large district, in the neighbor-hood of Twelfth street, in the South Division, unsupplied; for which it would be necessary to make some temporary provision, till the means can be obtained for erecting a house in that vicinity.

Another question which arises in view of all these facts is, whether it is not possible to construct our houses on a more economical plan? By erecting larger buildings, we can secure the same amount of room at very much less cost, and this the Board of Education has already recommended. It is possible that something may also be saved by adopting a still plainer style of architecture, and employing cheaper materials; but if this rule is applied to a much greater extent, I fear we shall receive few thanks from posterity for the buildings which we send down to them.

But whatever may be the *means* employed by the city for the accomplishment of the desired object, I take for granted that room will in some way be provided for the accommodation of the schools, as soon as our citizens can learn how urgent the necessities are.

The question is not, can we afford to provide accommodations for all the children that desire to attend the Public Schools, but rather, can we afford to leave a portion of them to grow up in ignorance and crime, and then prey upon the morals and wealth of the city. No man in his senses can doubt the *economy* even of furnishing the buildings required to bring these children under the healthful influences of the school room. It would be suicidal for us to pause in our efforts to provide for the education of the next generation.

The virtue and intelligence of any community are

its real life, without which all other possessions are worthless. On us rests the responsibility of deciding what shall be the character of this city one quarter of a century hence, and the influence that shall then control it. The history of the past is a pledge that this responsibility will be manfully and worthily met.

Of the 3,000 children in our city that do not attend any school, either public or private, it is safe to say that at least one thousand would have attended the public schools the last year, if suitable rooms had been provided to receive them.

In December, 1857, the whole number of pupils in attendance at the Foster school was 435. The new house in that district was opened in January, and in less than two months the number in attendance increased to 700.

But I need not urge these considerations. They are already understood and appreciated by a large portion of our citizens; and whenever public sentiment has been tested on this subject, it has always shown itself strongly enlisted in support of the public schools, and ready to meet all their reasonable wants.

HEATING AND VENTILATION.

The new houses that have been erected during the last three years, compare favorably with the best constructed school-houses in the country. They are not elaborately ornamented, but substantial and convenient.

In their arrangements for heating and ventilation, I regret to say, that some of them would hardly compare favorably with the poorest houses in the country. The greatest defects are found in the Ogden

School, which can never be satisfactorily warmed by the means now employed. The hot air furnaces have not sufficient capacity to warm a house of that size; and if they had twice their present capacity, they would never be able to warm the building with the present arrangement of hot air and cold air conductors. The cold air conductors have not more than one-fourth the capacity that is usually given to them in Boston and other eastern cities. The hot air conductors are not only too small, but they are greatly obstructed by unnecessary angles. One of the smoke-flues, also, is so much obstructed that it is impossible to secure the requisite draught; and both the furnaces are set so low that a vapor is constantly rising from water immediately under the fire, during a large portion of the winter.

In the High School it has been found necessary to introduce several stoves, in addition to the hot air furnaces; and in the Moseley School, the operation of the hot air furnaces is very imperfect. A similar difficulty exists in that portion of the Foster School which is warmed by hot air furnaces.

We come now to a question of vital importance — the comparative merits of the different systems of heating and ventilation. It is a reproach to the age in which we live, that with so many opportunities for advancement, we are, as yet, so far from having perfected anything like a satisfactory system of warming our houses, and furnishing them with a constant supply of pure air. Air that has been once breathed, is charged with a poisonous gas, and will not even support ordinary combustion. Any one desirous of satisfying himself on this point, can do so by the following simple experiment. Provide a vessel containing a few quarts of water, a short tube of sufficient size for the breath to pass freely through it, a common drinking glass, and a piece of candle about half an inch in length, attached to a few inches of wire, by which it may be suspended. Now plunge the glass into the water, and when the air is all expelled, invert and raise it gradually till most of the glass rises above the water; the open part being still below the surface, and the glass being still filled with the water. Next inhale a full breath of air and hold it in the lungs a few seconds; then breathe it through the tube under the edge of the glass. It will of course displace the water, and the glass will be filled with air from the lungs. Before taking the glass from the water, plunge in a small plate or board, and close the opening of the glass. It may now be set on a table and is ready for use. Having lighted the candle, remove the cover from the glass and drop the candle into the impure air, and the flame will be instantly extinguished.

To those who value the health of their children, it needs no argument to prove, that this de-vitalized, poisonous air should be constantly removed from the school room, and pure, life-giving air be introduced in its place. This important principle has not received sufficient attention in the construction of our new houses.

Hot air furnaces are natural ventilators. The heated air that is sent into the room by them, necessarily forces the same amount of impure air out of the room. But the heated air itself, with which the room is constantly supplied, is rendered more or less impure by contact with the heated surface of the furnace.

Having been familiar with the use of hot air furnaces for the last ten years, and having witnessed much more satisfactory results than we have been able to attain in the school houses of this city, my views have heretofore been decidedly in favor of this system of heating.

During the last year, I have devoted considerable attention to the different modes of heating by steam, and taken measures to ascertain the results of various experiments in steam-heating that have been tried in other cities.

In Boston, I found one of the largest school houses in the city very well *heated* by steam; but the *ventilation* was so defective, that the experiment was, on the whole, quite unsatisfactory. The radiators were all in the rooms to be warmed, and it was often found impossible to secure sufficient action in the ventilating flues. The Superintendent, in a recent letter, remarks, "As yet we have had no fair test of the comparative merits of the steam and hot air methods of heating, and my mind is not yet made up on the subject. In the three last large buildings, we have two plans for steam and one for hot air. In all, the original plans failed, and additional force has been supplied. The hot air one now has *seven* furnaces, which it is thought *may do*. With steam we have poor ventilation."

In Cincinnati, I examined a school building heated by steam, in which the radiators were placed in large boxes in the basement. These boxes were supplied by conductors with cold air, and the heated air passed by conductors into the different rooms, in the same manner as from an ordinary hot air furnace. A good ventilation was secured by this means, but some difficulty was experienced in securing the requisite degree of heat.

The Superintendent of Schools, for the city of New York, in reply to my enquiries on this subject, remarks, "The plan of heating our school buildings by furnaces, has, thus far; proved neither 'successful nor economical.' We have already had three buildings nearly burnt down, from some deficiency in the arrangement or construction of the pipes, within the past two months. The experiment of heating by steam has not yet been sufficiently tried to warrant any definite opinion on its merits."

In St. Louis, I found that an experiment had been tried in the use of steam, but it had proved a failure.

While these experiments have been going forward in other places, the Superintendent of Public Works in this city has introduced Blake, Wheelock & Co.'s Steam Heating Apparatus into one of our new buildings, and Perkins's Steam Heating Air Furnaces into the other. These experiments have been tried at the risk of the contractors, and the city has been protected against loss in case of failure. It is too soon to pronounce definitely upon the results of this test. The arrangements are not yet fully perfected, and the ventilators in both houses are much too small. I think we may, however, at this stage, safely say, that the city will be able to do better hereafter than to introduce any more hot air furnaces into our school buildings.

The steam apparatus of Blake, Wheelock & Co.,

which has been employed in the Brown School, has furnished a satisfactory amount of heat, with a moderate consumption of fuel. In cold days, when there is a great difference between the temperature of the outside and inside air, there has been little difficulty in securing a good degree of action in the ventilating flues, though the radiators are all placed in the rooms to be heated. In milder weather, when the difference between the temperature of the rooms and that of the outside air is inconsiderable, the ventilation is less satisfactory. •

The Perkins Apparatus, which is employed in one-half of the Foster School, has furnished a satisfactory supply of heated air of the purest quality; and as this air is forced into the room by the same means as that from hot air furnaces, a good action of the ventilating flues can always be secured. But the Perkins Apparatus, at the Foster School, has consumed much more fuel, in proportion to the space warmed, than the steam apparatus of Blake, Wheelock, & Co., at the Brown School. It is but justice to the agents of the Perkins Furnace to say, that this is the first school house which they have attempted to warm, and they do not regard the plan as perfected. They offer to increase the number of radiating tubes employed, and to guarantee that the whole building shall be satisfactorily warmed by the same furnaces that are now employed to warm only half of it.

HIGH SCHOOL.

Attendance.— As a general rule, there is no surer test of the efficiency of a school than its record of attendance. In the High Scdool, during the year

1857, the per cent. of attendance on the average number enrolled was ninety-six and six-tenths. The highest was during the session of two weeks, in July, when it rose to 99.4; and the lowest in March, when it was 95. If we make due allowance for sickness and other unavoidable causes of detention, we cannot expect a much higher standard than this.

The following is a list of those who were Perfect in their Attendance, being neither absent nor late during the year 1857:

WILLIAM H. ADAMS,	LAURA A. LEONARD,
JAMES E. BELL,	ALFRED L. LEADBEATER,
OLOF BENSON,	EMILY C. PETTY,
LLEWELLYN CHRISTIAN,	EDWARD F. PRICE,
GEORGE COOMBS,	JOHN RUTHERFORD,
MARY A. CORNELL,	LIZZIE SALTONSTAL,
MARY J. CRESWELL,	WILLIAM M. SCUDDER,
ALONZO J. CURRY,	WILLIAM C. SCUPHAM,
EDWARD H. CURTIS,	CHARLES M. STOW,
EDWARD C. HUBBARD,	A. HENRY VAN ZWOLL,
ELLEN A. HUBBARD,	EDWIN WALKER,
ELIZABETH B. HUNTLEY,	CAROLINE E. WRIGHT,
ALICE J. JENNINGS,	FREDERIC W. YOUSE.

Admissions.—It has not been found necessary to make any material change in the character of the examination for admission. It is believed that the method adopted continues to give general satisfaction. With the exception of Reading, the examinations are conducted entirely by means of written questions and answers. These answers are carefully preserved, and they are always open to the inspection of those who are interested in the results. No pains are spared to make the examinations just and impartial.

The following are the questions employed at the last examination:

ARITHMETIC.

1. In 144 miles, 1 furlong, 8 yards, 1 foot, how many feet?
2. Give a rule for the multiplication of decimals, and explain the method of "pointing off" in the following example: .0825 x .856.
3. What is the sum of $\frac{\frac{1}{4}}{6\frac{1}{4}}$ $\frac{3}{2\frac{1}{4}}$ $\frac{2\frac{1}{2}}{5\frac{1}{4}}$?
4. Reduce 35 rods, 9 feet and 2 inches to the fraction of a furlong.
5. Required the compound interest of $316 for 3 years, 4 months and 18 days, at six per cent.
6. A. has B.'s note for $914,75, due November 25, 1857; what is the note worth January 1, 1857?
7. Define ratio and proportion, and give examples of each.
8. A. sold a horse for $75 and lost 10 per cent.; what was its cost?
9. What is the square root of 776,161?
10. Give the table for wine measure.

GEOGRAPHY.

1. How do you reckon Longitude, and what is the value of a degree?
2. Give the political divisions of Europe.
3. Name the mountain chains of North America.
4. Name ten of the most important cities of South America, and give their location.
5. What groups of Islands east of Asia?
6. Name fifteen of the principal Rivers between the Alleghany and Rocky Mountains, and give their sources.
7. By what route would you travel from London to Calcutta?
8. What English and American settlements in Africa?
9. Between what parallels of latitude and what meridians does Australia lie?
10. Give what you know of the surface, soil and climate of Illinois.

GRAMMAR.

1. Define and name the vocals, sub-vocals and aspirates.
2. When, in the use of the indefinite article, do we employ the form "an," and when "a"? Do you say "an unit" or "a unit"—"such an one" or "such a one"?
3. Explain the difference between qualifying and limiting adjectives.
4. What do you understand by the "tense" of a verb? Give a synopsis of all the past perfect tenses of the verb "strike."
5. Give a full synopsis of the verbs "forsake," "lay," "work," "choose."
6. Analyze and parse the following sentence: "I was not aware of its being he."
7. Into what classes are conjunctions divided? Give examples of each.
8. Define each mode.
9. What is an abstract noun? What a collective noun? Give two or more sentences containing examples of each.

10. Correct the following sentences: "It was him;" "I don't write like you do;" Every one must judge of their own feelings;" "He shall not want for encouragement."

HISTORY.

1. Who were the Hessians?
2. Name the thirteen original states.
3. What can you say of Bacon's rebellion.
4. Give a brief account of King Philip's war.
5. What can you say of the early settlement of Maryland?
6. What were some of the first steps taken to promote education in the colonies?
7. What can you say of the first Colonial Congress?
8. What can you say of the Stamp Act?
9. What was the condition of the United States at the close of the Revolutionary War?
10. Give some account of the administration of Gen. Jackson.

SPELLING.

Courtesy,	Earnestness,	Fictitious,	Superficial,	Thoroughly,
Possession,	Philanthrophy,	Isthmus,	Guilty,	Reception,
Eagerness,	Vivacity,	Eccentric,	Mansion,	Prayer,
Fierce,	Reliance,	Atmosphere,	Guinea,	Scarcity.

The examination for admission was held July 9, 1857. The following table exhibits the result:

SCHOOLS.	Whole No. Examined.	Admitted.	Rejected.	Average Scholarship of whole No. Examined.
Dearborn School (No. 1)	27	8	19	56
Jones School (No. 2)	15	0	15	43
Scammon School (No. 3)	29	18	11	61
Kinzie School (No. 4)	8	2	6	52
Franklin School (No. 5)	5	0	5	46
Washington School (No. 6)	6	4	2	48
Moseley School (No. 7)	1	1	0	63
Brown School (No. 8)	2	0	2	51
Foster School (No. 9)	0	0	0	—
Ogden School (No. 10)	6	2	4	51
Summary from Public Schools	99	35	64	54
Private Schools	23	11	12	56
Total Summary	122	46	76	54

The next examination for admission to the High School will take place in July, 1858.

On the first of January, 1858, the whole number of pupils in the High School was 148. The number in the Classical Department was 64; in the English High Department, 68; in the Normal Department, 16.

The average age of the whole number was 16 years and 4 months. The average age of those in the Classical Department was 16 years and 3 months; in the English High, 15 years and 10 months; in the Normal, 18 years and 2 months.

The instructor in Modern Languages having resigned during the year, this department has been divided, and both French and German are now taught by native teachers. The number pursuing German at the present time is 61, and the class in French numbers 41.

Examinations.—Besides frequent reviews in all the different classes, the pupils are subjected to a thorough written examination at the close of the first and second terms of the year. At the end of the year, there is a public oral examination in all the studies pursued. This examination is continued for several days, and affords a favorable opportunity for parents and others to inform themselves in regard to the efficiency of the system of instruction, and the progress made by the pupils during the year. The design is to make the examination as thorough and searching as possible.

On the last day of the year, Public Anniversary Exercises are held, consisting of orations and essays by the pupils that have distinguished themselves during the year, by their successful devotion to study.

List of Pupils in the High School distinguished for Scholarship, Attendance and Deportment, during the year 1857, having Total Averages for the year not less than 94.

Normal Class.

Sophia J. Marshall,
Ann Winchell,

Alice J. Jennings,
Eliza C. Boyce.

Section A.

Fanny Wurts,
Edward F. Price,
A. Henry Van Zwoll,
Edwin Walker,
Ellen A. Hubbard,
Frederic W. Youse,
Alfred S. Wurts,

Morton Culver,
George H. Bliss,
George Throop,
Mary L. Herbert,
Martha P. Fennimore,
D. Emory Bradley.

Section B.

Edward H. Curtis,
William Throop,
Hugh Young,
Henry F. Chesbrough,
Edward H. Williams,
F. Pamelia Brown,
Ella C. Bradley,

J. Dearborn Haines,
Helen A. Leonard,
George H. Mendsen.
John Moore,
Marion Heald,
Sarah G. Downs.

Section C.

J. Sumter Chesbrough,
Elizabeth J. Saltonstall,

William M. Scudder.

Section D.

Brice A. Miller,
Olof Benson,
Eliza E. Ransom,
Cornelia G. Lunt,

Mary A. Cornell,
Michael Moore,
Clarence G. Peck,
Junius Simons.

Library.—Early in 1857, the $500, donated by Flavel Moseley, Esq., was expended in the purchase of suitable books for the High School Library; and cases have since been provided for their preservation. Some additions have been made to the number of volumes during the year. The library is indebted for numerous Public Documents to Hon. J. H. Woodworth, and to "A few Friends" for Johnson's Physical Atlas and other valuable works. The number of volumes in the library is 413.

' The following are the rules adopted in the distribution of books:

REGULATIONS.

ARTICLE 1. The Library shall be opened at the close of the afternoon session,
every Thursday in term time.

ART. 2. The Teachers of the High School may have access to the Library at
any time, and may draw books from it in accordance with articles 4 and 5.

ART. 3. Any pupil whose total average for any month shall equal or exceed
86, may draw books from the Library the ensuing month, and any whose average
shall equal or exceed 94, may have access to the Library at such times as the
Principal shall designate.

ART. 4. No folio, quarto or cyclopedia shall be taken from the Library, but
may be there consulted.

ART. 5. No one shall have more than one book from the Library at any time,
and no book shall be retained more than two weeks.

ART. 6. Any person injuring or losing any book belonging to the Library, shall
make compensation for the same, and failing to do so, shall be excluded from the
Library.

ART. 7. The Librarian shall keep an account of the names of all drawing
books from the Library; the numbers and names of the books, and the date of
drawing and returning.

ART. 8. The pupil having the highest total average for any month shall act as
Librarian for the succeeding month.

ART. 9. The Library shall be under the special care and supervision of the
Principal, subject to the direction of the Board of Education.

Course of Study.—No material change has been
made during the past year in the course of study.
The order of exercises cannot be fully and perma-
nently arranged till the school shall have been in
existence three years.

In a school containing both sexes and three distinct departments; requiring in some branches the
same course of instruction and in others an entirely
different one; where the pupils of one department
graduate in two years, those of another in three, and
those of another in four years, the question of classification and arrangement of studies is one requiring
much thought and labor.

3

A very serious obstacle to perfect classification, consists in the fact that a large part of the members of each class leave school before completing the full course. The same difficulty exists in all schools of a similar character. In the Philadelphia High School, which is one of the best in the country, more than one-half of the pupils leave before the expiration of two years. From the opening of the Chicago High School, October 8, 1856, to January 1, 1858, 28 per cent. of all admitted have left the school. This is a lower rate than in most schools of the kind.

When we consider these results, and reflect upon the changing character of our population and the attractions of business to young men in a city like this, it is evident that the High School has already gained a high place in the confidence and regard of our citizens; and there is much reason to hope that the leading object of the school, that of furnishing to the city annually a class of young men and women of superior education and intelligence, will not fail of success.

When a pupil is admitted to the school, the following Circular is immediately addressed to the parent, explaining the scope and direction of the different departments of study:

CHICAGO HIGH SCHOOL, }
——, 185 }

DEAR SIR: Your —— having passed the requisite examination, is admitted as a pupil of the Chicago High School.

The Board of Education, desiring to give the children of their fellow-citizens as complete a course of instruction as possible, in the time devoted to this object, and to adapt the character of the instruction to the intended pursuit of the student in after life, have arranged as follows the studies of the school:

1. THE CLASSICAL COURSE. — This extends through three years and includes all the studies pursued in the school, except the more advanced English

branches, such as the Higher Mathematics, Chemistry, etc. It is recommended to all who intend to give their children a Collegiate education, or who design them for Teachers, or for any other occupation or profession in which an acqaintance with the Ancient Languages is deemed desirable.

2. THE ENGLISH HIGH COURSE.—This extends through three years, and includes all the studies taught in the school, except the Ancient Languages. It is recommended to all who design their children for pursuits connected with trade, commerce, manufacture and the mechanic arts.

3. THE CLASSICAL AND ENGLISH HIGH COURSE.—This extends through four years, and includes all the studies taught in the school. It is recommended to all who intend continuing their children in school four years.

4. THE NORMAL COURSE. — This extends through two years, and is intended for young ladies desiring to become Teachers.

You are respectfully requested to select from these Courses the one you wish your ——— to pursue. The students of the different courses, admitted at the same time, form but one class in most of their studies.

Whichever course you select, your ——— will have the same advantages of general discipline, moral culture and companionship.

Respectfully,

CHARLES A. DUPEE, *Principal.*

Records and Reports.—All the recitations are graded on a scale from 0 to 100, and a permanent record is made of the standing of each pupil. This exhibits, in a definite form, the progress of the pupils during their connection with the schools. Similar records in other cities are consulted as *criteria* of the character and ability of graduates, by those who wish to employ them in business, or for other reasons desire to obtain a correct idea of their character and capacity.

At the close of every month, a report of the standing of each pupil is sent to the parent or guardian. The following is the form of this report:

CHICAGO HIGH SCHOOL.

Report of .... *No.* .... *in Section* ...... *consisting of* .... *Pupils in the* .... *Department, for the Term ending* 185

	1st Month.	2d Month.	3d Month.	4th Month.	Examination Average	Average for Term.
Scholarship Average,						
Deportment Average,						
Attendance Average,						
Total Average,						

PARENT'S SIGNATURE.

Scholarship, Attendance and Deportment are graded from 100 to 0. The average of the daily recitations in each study for the month constitutes the Scholarship Average. The averages of the daily attendance and deportment for the month constitute the Attendance and Deportment Averages. The Examination Average for the Term is regarded as equivalent to the average for one month. The average of all these results for the Term is the Total Average, and constitutes the pupil's rank for the Term.

The parent is respectfully requested to examine the accompanying report and, after appending his signature, to return it by the bearer.

CHARLES A. DUPEE, *Principal.*

Habits of Study.—The formation of correct habits of study is a subject that deserves special consideration. With the view of correcting certain evils that are liable to arise, the following Circular is addressed by the Principal of the School to the parent of each pupil:

CHICAGO HIGH SCHOOL, ⎫
——, 185　　　 ⎭

DEAR SIR: Your coöperation is respectfully requested in our endeavors to regulate the time devoted by your ———— to study.

Our daily session, of but five hours, being necessarily occupied, for the most part, with recitations and miscellaneous exercises, less than an hour and a half a day can be employed in school in the preparation of lessons. It is evident that seven hours a week is totally insufficient to secure any real progress in studies, or any proper intellectual development. Hence every pupil is expected to devote considerable time to study out of school. Two hours and a half a day is recommended as the time which the pupil should employ in study out of school.

While the faithful teacher cannot, by his unaided efforts, at once inspire all his pupils with a suitable devotion to study, neither can he discharge his duty without awakening in many an interest which, without proper supervision, will sometimes lead to evil results. Pupils, desirous of improving the advantages afforded them, become ambitious to excel, and, if uncontrolled, sometimes imprudently devote time and labor to the preparation of studies, at a sacrifice of health.

We shall exercise great care that all lessons assigned may be prepared, by reasonable exertion, in the time which can judiciously be devoted to study. The time actually consumed in the preparation of lessons does not, however, depend altogether, nor mainly, upon their length.

For instance, a lesson is assigned which might be thoroughly prepared, by concentrated effort, in an hour and a half. One pupil, excessively anxious to render it absolutely certain that he is thoroughly informed on all points in the lesson, will employ several hours on the same subject, without any positive advantage, and with loss of time, strength and mental discipline.

Another devotes to the task several hours of desultory effort, interrupted in numberless ways, with a great sacrifice of time and all that power of concentrated, disciplined effort which a suitable education aims to establish.

Another, neglecting his duties day and evening, commences his labor at a late hour, and continues it till after midnight. Few pupils can study, with advantage, later than nine o'clock at night, and none, without injury, later than ten o'clock. Indeed, all of these methods are greatly to be deprecated, as destructive of health, systematic habits, and mental discipline. It may be added, that the student who expects to prosecute his studies with any efficiency can devote but little time, during a term, to parties or other social pleasures which imply late hours and a great expenditure of time.

While we would, therefore, urge the necessity of your ———— devoting considerable time to study, out of school, daily, we would especially request you to exercise such supervision as will prevent this duty from encroaching upon the time which should be devoted to physical exercise and rest.

Very respectfully,

CHARLES A. DUPEE, *Principal.*

GRAMMAR AND PRIMARY SCHOOLS.

Instruction.—The Grammar Schools of the city are doing their appropriate work in a thorough and satisfactory manner. The chief impediment in the way of their success, is the lack of suitable accommodations that still exists in most of the houses.

The Primary Schools are doing quite as well as it is reasonable to expect, after making due allowance for the crowded condition of the rooms, and the small number of teachers in proportion to the number of scholars; but is painfully true that, in some cases, this allowance cannot be regarded as less than one-half of the effective power and influence of the school. This evil is greater in several of the schools at the present time than it was a year ago, and unless some remedy can be speedily provided, it will be vain to expect any satisfactory progress in the Primary Schools. Even in the new buildings, in which the number of seats and desks is designedly limited to the number of pupils that one teacher can properly instruct, it has often been found necessary to break up the system, by introducing benches around the walls of the room, for the accommodation of additional scholars.

As this is now the greatest evil with which we

have to contend, I have made some effort to ascertain how our schools compare, in this respect, with those of other cities. The average number of pupils assigned to each teacher, in the Grammar and Primary Schools of all the cities from which I have reliable information, is as follows:

Buffalo..46
Cincinnati...49
New York..50
St. Louis...50
Cleveland...54
Philadelphia......................................55
Boston..57
Chicago...78

There can be no doubt that Chicago employs the smallest number of teachers in proportion to the number of children belonging to the schools, of any city in the Union. The city of Buffalo, with a population of about 90,000, employs more than one hundren and eighty teachers in the Grammar and Primary Schools, and Chicago employs less than eighty. The whole amount paid in Buffalo for teachers' wages, during the last year, was more than twice the whole amount paid in Chicago. This evil has not arisen from a lack of disposition on the part of the Board of Education to furnish a suitable number of teachers, but from the fact that there were no rooms in which additional teachers could be placed, if they were appointed.

No principle in didactics is more fully settled than that any increase above sixty in the number of pupils assigned to a single teacher, necessarily involves a corresponding loss in the efficiency of instruction. In many cities, the maximum number is placed as low as fifty, and in some as low as forty-five. There are, at the present time, several teachers in our own schools, each of whom is made responsible for the sole instruction of one hundred and fifty children.

In the Primary Schools, a few modifications have been introduced, during the last year, in the course of instruction. All the children now have exercises on the slate or blackboard, more or less frequent, in which some attention is given to the elements of drawing and writing. Another improvement has been the introduction of "Object Lessons," or "Lessons on Common Things." Laying aside the formality of an ordinary recitation, some common object, as a book or a pencil, is brought before the school, and made the subject of familiar conversation between the teacher and her pupils. The object of these "Developing Exercises," is to give the pupils clear and accurate ideas of the nature and relations of common objects around them, and also to give them such power of expression that they will be able to clothe these ideas in appropriate language.

In several of the schools, there has been a decided improvement in the manner of teaching the elementary sounds of the language, and the effect has already manifested itself in a corresponding improvement in teaching the elements of Reading.

The general progress of the pupils in the Grammar Schools has been much greater than in the Primary, for the reason that, in proportion to the number of scholars, they have had more room or more teachers. It is believed that a large class will be found qualified to enter the High School at the next examination, in July.

It is desirable that more attention should be paid, in most of the Grammar Schools, to spelling. But the branch which appears to be most unsatisfactorily taught in any of the schools, is Penmanship; while it is equally true, that in some of the schools no branch is better taught than this. If a teacher of Penmanship could be employed, who should pass from school to school, and devote all his time to this branch, it would unquestionably be a great improvement upon our present system.

Lessons in Vocal Music have been given once a week in all the schools. This department is under the direction of a faithful and competent instructor, and the progress of the pupils has been as great as could be expected from the time devoted to this branch.

Discipline.—In the general government of the schools, some progress has been made during the year. The discipline of the pupils is as good now as it was a year ago, and in several of the schools the amount of corporeal punishment has been very considerably reduced. There are others in which no such improvement has been made. I trust I shall be pardoned for saying, that notwithstanding the unfavorable condition of the rooms, I believe the amount of punishment may yet be reduced in some of the schools, and especially in the Primary Departments, one-half at least, without affecting unfavorably the discipline of the classes.

The principals of several of the schools have adopted the plan of having a record preserved of all the punishments inflicted by each teacher, with very gratifying results.

Attendance.—The greatest improvement that has been made in the Grammar and Primary Schools during the last year, is in the attendance of the pupils.

NEW RULE.

The evil of irregular attendance is one that has long engaged the attention of the Board of Education, and one that has hitherto baffled all the efforts that have been made for its removal. It is now universally regarded as the most dangerous evil that exists in connection with the free school system.

Near the close of 1857, the Board adopted the following rule, which took effect on the first of January, 1858:

"Any scholar who shall be absent six half days in four consecutive weeks, without an excuse from the parent or guardian, given either in person or by written note, satisfying the teacher that the absences were caused by his own sickness or by sickness in the family, shall forfeit his seat in the school; and the teacher shall forthwith notify the parent and the Superintendent that the pupil is suspended. No pupil thus suspended shall be restored to school, till he has given satisfactory assurance of punctuality in the future, and obtained permission from the Superintendent to return."

The propriety or impropriety of adopting such a rule, involves grave questions, which lie at the very foundation of our system of free schools.

That education should be free and universal, is now the prevailing sentiment of this nation. The primary basis on which the doctrine of free schools rests, is the safety of the State. Uneducated men and women are regarded as a dangerous element in a free Republic. There are, however, many who still look with distrust upon schools entirely free, and the number would be found to be much larger than it appears, if it were not for the odium of entertaining sentiments that are unpopular with the masses. Even among the ablest and most devoted friends of popular education, there are not wanting those who regard it as unwise to make our schools entirely free to children whose parents are able to contribute to their support. They believe that opportunities which cost nothing can never be fully appreciated, and that our schools can never rise to the highest order of excellence while those who enjoy their benefits do not put forth any direct effort to aid in sustaining them. The Hon. Henry Barnard, of Connecticut, one of the ablest and most devoted friends of education in the country, has long entertained this view of the subject. During the last year, an animated discussion on this question took place on New England ground, between Mr. Barnard and the Hon. George S. Boutwell, Secretary of the Massachusetts Board of Education.

The friends of free schools have much to fear from the arguments that are based upon the irregular attendance of scholars, and the consequent waste of so large a portion of the funds that are provided for the support of the schools. If this waste was as apparent as it is real, a remedy in some form would long since have been demanded.

Let us take, for illustration, our own city. The average number of absences from all the Grammar and Primary Schools during the year, was more than one-fifth of the average number belonging to the schools. But if one-fifth of the children are alway absent, there is an absolute loss of one-fifth of the expense of sustaining the schools, for it is obviously much easier to instruct any number of pupils that are punctual, than the same number that are habitually irregular in their attendance. The derangement of classes and the time required to bring up lost lessons, are always more than an equivalent for the time saved by any reduction of numbers that may be occasioned by absences. Here, then, is a positive loss to the city of more than $12,000 during the year 1857. In two years, this loss amounts to a sum sufficient to build one of our first class school houses.

But it is not the waste of money alone, that is sapping the foundations of our free school system. One of the principal objects in making the schools free and common to all classes, is to remove the danger of having an uneducated and vicious class of persons constantly growing up, to prey upon society. This object is of course in a great degree lost, if those whom the schools are desired to raise from vagrancy and ignorance, are to regard them with indifference and neglect.

In this city, as in others, there is a class of parents who seem to regard the public schools as convenient places, where they may send their children on days when they happen to have nothing else for them to do. The consequence is, that many children have been in the habit of attending school only one or two days in the week—in some instances not more than two or three days in a month; often enough to retard the progress of the class with which they were connected, but not often enough to derive any substantial benefit themselves. *

---

* The following is an extract from a late Report of H. H. BARNEY, Esq., Commissioner of Common Schools, for the State of Ohio:

"The annual school reports from County Auditors disclose the fact, that the

But there is another evil connected with the irregular attendance of scholars, that is seriously affecting the interests of free schools. The absence of a portion of a class, retards the progress of all the rest. It is safe to say that in many of the classes in our schools, the advancement has not been more than two-thirds or three-fourths as great as it would have been if the pupils had been punctual in their attendance. If all the members of a class were equally irregular, each pupil would suffer his own share of this loss. But the records of the schools show that more than one-half of the absences belong to less than one-fifth of the scholars. Here, then, is a most glaring injustice. Parents sometimes claim that they have a right to keep their children from school when they please, without stopping to consider that other parents, whose children are uniformly punctual, have

---

average yearly attendance of the scholars in our common schools is less than two-thirds of the average number enrolled or belonging to the schools. It is conceded by every experienced teacher and school officer, that the expense of a school is not diminished by the circumstance that the average daily attendance of its pupils is less than the number belonging to it; in other words, that it costs no more to instruct a school of forty-five scholars, all of whom attend regularly, than it would if the average daily attendance were only one-half of the number enrolled. Indeed, it is fully believed by teachers who have tried the experiment, that a school enrolling sixty scholars, all of whom attend regularly, in charge of a single-teacher, will make greater proficiency than if the average daily attendance were only forty-five.

"Hence it is easy to see, that in consequence of irregular attendance, not only one-third of all the school funds annually raised and distributed for the payment of teachers, is lost, actually thrown away, but one-third part of the time allowed for the cultivation of the minds of the youth of the State, is also lost. To the account then of irregularity of attendance, the annual loss of half a million of dollars may be justly charged.

"But this most lamentable waste of money is but an atom in the scale, when weighed against *neglected opportunities, misspent time, and the formation of evil habits.*"

also a right to expect that they will not be kept back in their classes by those who are habitually irregular.

Heretofore this right of the few to hinder the progress of the many, has been yielded; while the right of the many to advance without these impediments, has been disregarded. A large portion of the children that are taken from the public schools and placed under private instruction, are transferred from this cause; while many of the parents whose children still remain, have an abiding feeling that their rights are disregarded for the gratification of those who are indifferent to the education of their own children.

Every one at all conversant with our schools, is aware that most of the absences that occur, are occasioned by the carelessness and neglect of parents, and not by any real necessity.

If this evil is to continue unchecked, our schools can never reach a high standard of excellence, and many parents will contrive to send their children to private schools, rather than submit to the annoyance of having them classed with those who have no ambition to improve, and who are not willing to put forth the necessary effort to establish habits of punctuality.

On the other hand, if the *rights of all* shall be equally regarded, and an ordinary degree of regularity in attendance upon the schools shall be made a condition of membership, then may we expect that our schools will continue to advance, and become more and more worthy of the confidence of all classes in the community.

I have taken the liberty to present these views, because it is vain for us to close our eyes against evils that threaten the stability of our noble system of public instruction. I believe that this system is destined to triumph, and that, in the future history of the country, the common schools will be entirely free. But of nothing do I feel more fully assured than this, that if the free school system is finally to prevail, it must be by reducing it to a rigidly economical basis, and by treating the rights of all with equal consideration.

It was with this view of the case, that the Board of Education adopted the rule requiring those who enter the public schools of this city, to attend with some degree of regularity. The rule has already accomplished twice as much in improving the standard of punctuality in our schools, as all previous agencies combined.

So far as I can learn, the rule has given general satisfaction. More than a hundred different parents have already applied in person to have their children restored to the seats that had been forfeited by irregular attendance; but I can recollect only a single instance in which a parent has made any special complaint of the rule itself, while in a large majority of cases, those whom I have seen have expressed themselves gratified with its adoption.

It is not the design of the rule to exclude from the schools any children whose parents put forth sufficient effort to secure an ordinary degree of punctuality; and even when a seat has been forfeited, the pupil is not necessarily deprived of the privileges of the school, except for a single day.

One of the most important advantages of the rule, is the opportunity it affords the Superintendent to confer with parents in regard to the interests of their children and of the schools.

Similar rules have already been adopted in St. Louis, Dubuque, Cincinnati, Hartford, New Haven, Worcester, and other cities; embracing the principle that habitual irregularity of attendance is a sufficient cause for depriving a pupil of his seat in school.

The Board of Visitors of the City of Hartford, in their Annual Report, remark:

" After much patient deliberation and correspondence with other cities, where the same evil had existed and been remedied; and after having advised with the best friends of education, and the best legal authority in the State, the Board adopted the following rule, viz. :

" In all the departments of the District Schools, except the Primary, pupils who have been absent five sessions since the last regular entrance day, for any cause, save sickness, or death of friends, shall not be allowed to enter again until the next regular entrance day, unless bringing a written permit from one of the Acting School Visitors."

After stating that, in several of the largest schools of the city, the effect of this rule has been to reduce the number of absences from one-third to one-half, the visitors add:

" These statements will at once present the results of the rule, and, we think, fully demonstrate the necessity and wisdom of the action of the Board in its adoption."

The Board of Visitors of the City of New Haven, in their Annual Report, remark:

" The practice of dismissing from school any pupil who is absent from his place five or six half days, without an excuse satisfactory to the Acting Visitor, has had a most excellent effect, and chiefly for the reason that it has brought the parent, who is generally most in fault, to the Committee, where mutual explanations and pledges have restored the pupil to the school."

In St. Louis, the following rule has been in operation in the Public Schools for several years, and I learn, by a recent communication from the Superintendent, that the effect has been salutary:

" Any pupil who shall be absent four half days in one month, or who is repeatedly tardy, without giving a written excuse satisfactory to the teacher, may be suspended from the school by the teacher, written notice of which shall be immediately given to the parent or guardian, and to the Superintendent."

Summary View.—The attendance records of the Grammar and Primary Schools, for the years 1856 and 1857, present the following results:

	1857.			1856.
	BOYS.	GIRLS.	BOTH.	BOTH.
Whole number of different scholars enrolled...............	5,876	4,760	10,636	8,542
Average number belonging....	2,414	1,904	4,318	3,688
Average daily attendance......	1,893	1,461	3,354	2,606
Per cent. of daily attendance on whole number enrolled...	32	31	31.5	31
Per cent. of daily attendance on average number belonging...	77.5	77	77	71

The following table exhibits the *per cent. of average attendance* in the several Grammar and Primary schools, *on the average number belonging*, for the years 1856 and 1857:

SCHOOLS.	1856.			1857.		
	Gram. Dep.	Prim. Dep.	Both.	Gram. Dep.	Prim. Dep.	Both.
Dearborn School (No. 1).....	82	81	81	85	70	75
Jones School (No. 2)........	80	63	69	85	75	78
Scammon School (No. 3).....	85	70	76	91	74	81
Kinzie School (No. 4)........	81	58	69	81	73	75
Franklin School (No. 5)......	80	63	70	83	74	79
Washington School (No. 6)...	79	66	70	·74	66	69
Moseley School (No. 7)......	63	63	63	88	78	80
Brown School (No. 8).......	75	69	71	87	80	82.5
Foster School (No. 9)........	69	64	66	85	78	80
Ogden School (No. 10)......				90	79	83
Average of all the Schools...	80	66	71	85	73	77
Average No. belonging.			3688	1495	2823	4318
Average No. attending......			2606	1272	2082	3354

4

The whole number of different scholars in 1857, including those
    of the High School, was..............................10,786
Whole number in 1856..................................8,577
Whole number in 1855..................................6,826
Increase in 1856.......................................1,751
Increase in 1857. 2,209

CURVES OF ATTENDANCE.

The accompanying Plate has been prepared with much care, and presents a distinct view of the fluctuations of enrolment and attendance, in the Grammar and Primary Schools, during the year 1857.

The distance of any point in the upper curve from the base line, represents the number enrolled at that time as members of the schools, on a scale of 2000 pupils to an inch.

The distance of any point in the lower curve from the base line, shows the number actually attending the schools, at that date.

The Curve of Enrolment commences in January far below the average enrolment for the year. During the first three weeks, it rises very gradually; but during the last week in January and nearly the whole of February, it rises rapidly, passing the point of average enrolment for the year, about the 20th of February. The highest point in the term is reached about the 1st of April; and after this time it sinks rapidly, reaching a point below the average for the year before the close of the term.

The enrolment of the second term commences higher than that of the first, and closes lower.

The enrolment of the third term commences, in September, about the same as that at the beginning of the year, and rises constantly till about the 10th of November. It then sinks for about two weeks, after which it rises rapidly, and reaches the highest point of the year about the middle of December.

CURVES OF ATTENDANCE AND ENROLMENT OF SCHOLARS IN THE PUBLIC SCHOOLS. CHICAGO. 1857

January	February	March	April	May	June	July	September	October	November	December
Aver. Attend. 2881	3299	3367	3282	3188	3324	2894	3251	3583	3585	4236

1857 Average Enrolment 3348

1857 Average Attendance 3354

Incr. Attendance 2606

March Culmination

Spring Vacation

Curve of actual Enrolment 1857

Curve of actual Attendance 1857

Summer Vacation

Dec. Culm.

Base line of the Curves

The distance of any point in either curve, from the base in 2000ths of an inch shows the aver. No of Scholars belonging (or attending) for the corresponding date

Line of increase of Scholars in the Chicago Public Schools for 1857 - 47 Per Ct.

	1856	1857
Average No of Scholars Belonging.	3685	4818
Attending.	2606	3354
Pr.Ct. of Attend Gram. Pop.	80	85
Primary Dep.	66	73
both Departments.	71	77

The Curve of Attendance is much more irregular than the Curve of Enrolment.

The average distance of the two curves from the base line, and from each other, during the first and second terms, shows that the absences for this portion of the year were about one-fourth of the number belonging to the schools.

During the last two weeks of the second term, in July, the attendance falls off very rapidly, and, at the close of the term, reaches the lowest point of the year.

During the third term, the two curves are found much nearer together than on either of the preceding terms, showing a marked improvement in the attendance of the pupils during the Autumn term.

The highest per cent. of attendance was in December, when there were more scholars than at any other time in the year; and the lowest was in July, when the number enrolled was considerably below the average for the year.

In December, the average distance of the curves from each other is about fourteen-hundredths of the distance from the Curve of Enrolment to the base line, making the average attendance of the schools for this month about 86 per cent., while the average attendance for the year was only 77 per cent.

The severe weather experienced during a portion of November, has left a corresponding depression in the Curve of Attendance for that month.

Monthly Report to Parents.—A rule has recently been adopted by the Board of Education, making it the duty of the teachers in the Grammar Schools to send a Monthly Report to the parent or guardian of each pupil, showing the averages of the pupil in attendance, scholarship and deportment, to be signed by the parent or guardian, and returned to the teacher.

The following is the form that has been adopted:

.... SCHOOL, CHICAGO.

Monthly Report of .... *a Member of the* .... *Class, in the* .... *Division, for the Term commencing* .... 1858.

MONTH ENDING	ATTENDANCE.				Attendance Average.	Scholarship Average.	Deportment Average.	General Average.	General Average of the Class.	SIGNATURE OF PARENT OR GUARDIAN.
	Punctual.	Late.	Dismissed.	A b						

☞ The highest degree of excellence is denoted by the number 100. The column marked *General Average* combines the the three averages of *Attendance*, *Scholarship* and *Deportment*, and shows the general standing of the pupil. Each tardiness, or dismissal before the close of the school, deducts 1 from 100 in the *Attendance Average*, and each absence deducts 2; but absences occasioned by sickness do not affect either the *Attendance Average* or the *General Average*. The last column is introduced for the purpose of showing whether the standing of the pupil is above or below the *General Average* of the whole class.

☞ The parent or guardian is respectfully requested to examine and sign this report each month, and return it by the bearer.

           ————, *Principal.*

VISITS FROM PARENTS.

In my last Report, I sent out a special request, in behalf of the schools, that parents would visit them at least once every term. A careful record of the visits received during the year 1857 was preserved in all the schools, with the following results:

In the Dearborn School, the number of visits from parents and
  guardians, during the year, was......................... 94
In the Jones School... 80
In the Scammon School...................................... 45
In the Kinzie School.. 11
In the Franklin School...................................... 11
In the Washington School.................................... 7
In the Moseley School....................................... 60
In the Brown School..116
In the Foster School.. 8
In the Ogden School... 75

Whenever parents have brought complaints of teachers to this office, I have ascertained, on inquiry, in almost every instance, that they had never visited the teachers complained of, except, perhaps, to carry the same complaint there. They have seemed to be wholly unconscious that, while charging the teachers with blame, they were themselves guilty of inexcusabe neglect.

It certainly cannot be impracticable for parents to encourage the schools by spending at least one hour each term in witnessing the progress of their children. This has not been done during the past year by one parent in fifty of those whose children attend the public schools.

There will be a public examination of all the schools during the Spring term, of which parents and others will receive due notice through the pupils.

UNEDUCATED CHILDREN.

Unless the number of children of suitable age to attend school increased much faster in 1857 than it did in 1856, the number of children in the city who do not attend any school, either public or private, has very considerably diminished during the last year.

The whole number of pupils of school age attending the private schools during the year 1857, is ascertained by careful census to have been about 4,500. This is quite as large as the number attending private schools during 1856. But the increase in the whole number of scholars attending the public schools in 1857 was 2209, while the increase in 1856 was only 1751.

CHANGE OF NAMES.

At a meeting of the Board of Education, February 27, 1858, Mr. Haven, Chairman of the Committee appointed to consider the expediency of changing the names by which the public schools were designated, presented the following report:

To the Board of Education of the City of Chicago:

GENTLEMEN: Your Committee to whom was referred the question of presenting to this Board appropriate names for our several Grammar Schools, have had the matter under consideration, and beg leave to Report:

That in the opinion of your Committee, a better method than the one now in use for designating our several Grammar Schools, should be at once adopted. With only the present number of schools, members of this Board, even, familiar as they are with the subject, often find it difficult to locate a particular school by its number; and as our schools must rapidly increase, the difficulty of recognition, and of retaining their locations in the memory, by their numbers, must be greatly augmented. But, by giving to each school some appropriate name, association comes to the aid of memory, and the location of every school is readily known and easily retained, not only by members of this Board, but by our citizens generally, when once its name is learned.

It has been the aim of your Committee to present such names for our several schools as should approve themselves to the minds of all. Some of them have a national character, known and honored everywhere; others were early and honorably connected with the first settlement of our city; others still have shown their appreciation of the value of our Public Schools by giving liberally of their time or their means, or both, to make them what they are now fast becoming — the ornament and pride of the city.

With these views, the Committee ask for the passage of the following resolution:

Resolved, That our several Grammar Schools be known, hereafter, by the following names, viz.:

No. 1, as Dearborn.	No. 6, as Washington.
No. 2, as Jones.	No. 7, as Moseley.
No. 3, as Scammon.	No. 8, as Brown.
No. 4, as Kinzie.	No. 9, as Foster.
No. 5, as Franklin.	No. 10, as Ogden.

The foregoing report was accepted, and the resolution adopted.

SCHOOL APPARATUS.

The High School has now been in operation one year and a half, and a portion of the pupils will complete their course of study the next term; but the inventory of apparatus that has thus far been provided to illustrate the different branches of science, is limited to a supply of blackboards and chalk. The whole value of the maps, globes, and other apparatus belonging to the Grammar and Primary Schools of the city, does not exceed $25. It is safe to say that there cannot be found another city of even 50,000 inhabitants, with so scanty a supply of apparatus in the public schools.

It is impossible for the High School to furnish satisfactory instruction in such branches as Chemistry, Natural Philosophy, Astronomy and Surveying, without the aid of appropriate apparatus; and the Grammar and Primary Schools greatly need a supply of outline maps, globes, etc.

TEACHERS INSTITUTE.

The teachers of the public schools meet at the High School on the second Saturday of every month, and devote the forenoon to exercises designed for their mutual improvement in the theory and practice of teaching.

The Institute was established by the Board of Education, and a regular attendance at the meetings is one of the conditions on which the teachers receive their appointments in the schools. It affords opportunity for the Superintendent to communicate freely with the teachers on all matters of general interest in relation to the schools; and the teachers here become better acquainted with one another, and learn each other's views and modes of discipline and instruction. Model classes are presented from the different schools, and a great variety of practical questions relating to the duties of the school room are freely and familiarly discussed.

There has been a full and punctual attendance at these meetings the past year, and the interest of the exercises has been well sustained. It is due to the ladies to say, that they have met their full proportion of the labor and responsibility. The essays that have appeared monthly in the pages of the "Chicago Teacher," would compare favorably with those of more pretending educational Journals.

As another evidence of the professional character and interest of the teachers in the public schools, it may be mentioned in this connection, that a large majority of them are subscribers to the Illinois Teacher, and several are also subscribers to Barnard's Journal of Education, the largest and most comprehensive educational periodical in existence.

MOSELEY FUND.

In 1856, a Fund of $1,000 was established by Flavel Moseley, Esq., the interest of which is expended in the purchase of text-books for indigent ·children attending the public schools. During the first year, the income of this Fund, ($120), was found sufficient to meet the wants of all who were entitled to the benefit of it; but the number of indigent children attending the schools has greatly increased, and it has already been found necessary to obtain by private subscriptions the sum of $120 to add to the income of the Fund, for present use. Twelve gentlemen have generously contributed $10 each for this object. But notwithstanding the timely aid thus rendered, the resources of the Fund are now nearly exhausted, and it is highly important that some permanent provision should be made for meeting the increased necessities of this class of children.

FOSTER MEDALS.

One year ago, Doctor John H. Foster established a Fund of $1,000, the avails of which are to be expended in procuring medals and other rewards of merit for the most deserving pupils attending the Grammar Schools of the city. The first award of medals is to be made at the close of the r · term, in July.

JONES FUND.

It is my privilege again to record the munificence of one of our philanthropic citizens, in establishing an additional Fund in aid of the public schools. William

Jones, Esq., a gentleman who has long taken a deep interest in the schools, and who was for many years Chairman of the Board of Inspectors, has placed at the disposal of the Board of Education the sum of $1,000, the interest of which is to be applied for the benefit of the Jones School, in procuring text-books for indigent children, books of reference, maps, globes, etc.

TERMS AND VACATIONS.

The terms of the Public Schools commence on the second day of January, the Monday after the last Friday in April, and the first Monday in September; and close two weeks before the last Friday in April, the second Friday in July, and the twenty-fourth day of December: *Provided*, That when the second day of January occurs later in the week than Wednesday, then the schools do not commence till the following Monday.

SCHOOL FUND.

The amount of real estate now belonging to the school fund,
within the limits of the city, is estimated at...........$900,000
Amount of real estate outside of the city................. 25,000
Money loaned, principal............................... 52,000

Whole amount of school fund....................$977,000

A considerable portion of the real estate belonging to this fund is not now available, and much of it is leased on very low rents.

Block 87, of the school section, is leased to the city for the nominal sum of $800 per annum, till December, 1862. The adjoining block, 88, is leased to private parties for $8,500 per annum. In the present straitened condition of the School Tax Fund, it is to be hoped that the city will recognize the justice of paying to the School Fund a fair rent for this property.

The High School, the Scammon School, and the Jones School, are all situated on lots belonging to the School Fund, and not to the city. If these lots were leased to the city for school purposes, the rent received by the School Fund would be paid by the School Tax Fund, so that the schools would derive no real benefit; but as it is a plain violation of the City Charter to appropriate the avails of the School Fund to any other purpose than the payment of teachers, it seems desirable to take such measures as may be necessary to correct this irregularity.

The income of the School Fund, for the year ending February 1, 1858, including also the dividend of interest on the State Fund, was as follows:

Interest on $52,000, loaned........................	$6,240.00
Rents..	11,648.50
State dividend....................................	18,255.60
Amount.......................................	$36,144.10
The amount paid by this fund, for salaries of teachers, school agent, and superintendent, was....................	36,079.18
Balance.......................................	$64.92

The rents received by the School Fund during the current year will be about $6,700 more than those of the last year; and if the city should estimate the rent of block 87, of the school section, at its true value, there would be a further addition of at least $7,000.

EXPENDITURES FOR THE SUPPORT OF SCHOOLS.

The whole expense of supporting the Public Schools, during the year ending February 1, 1858, may be reduced to three general heads:

1. Salaries of Teachers, School Agent and Superintendent, paid by the school fund.............................$36,079
2. Incidentals, including fuel, repairs, care of buildings, office expenses, printing, etc............................. 9,622
3. Rent of school houses, including interest on buildings and lots belonging to the city, estimated.................. 17,000

Amount..$62,701

This amount, divided by 10786, the whole number of pupils instructed, shows the expense for each scholar to have been $5.81.

The following is the comparative cost of instruction in several different cities, reduced to the basis here adopted for Chicago:

Boston,   for each pupil taught.......................$13.00
St. Louis,   "   " 11.11
Cincinnati, "   " 9.57
Providence, "   " 9.00
Cleveland,   "   " 8.69
Philadelphia, "   " 8.55
New York,   "   " 6.50
Buffalo,   "   " 6.32
Chicago,   "   " 5.81

This list embraces all the principal cities from which I have been able to obtain reliable information; and the statistics from which the results are obtained have been scanned and reduced with more than ordinary care.

If any one is desirous of learning whether the Public Schools of Chicago were *economically* conducted during the year ending February 1, 1858, he will here find a satisfactory answer to his inquiries.

W. H. WELLS,
Superintendent of Public Schools.
Chicago, March 20, 1858.

APPENDIX.

BOARD OF EDUCATION.

SUPERINTENDENT OF PUBLIC SCHOOLS

W. H. WELLS.

Office, 64 Lake street, up stairs; House, 342 West Madison street.

SCHOOLS, TEACHERS AND SALARIES.

CHICAGO HIGH SCHOOL,

Monroe street, between Halstead and Des Plaines.

Charles A. Dupee, Principal....................................$2,000
Leander H. Potter.. 1,000
Edward C. Delano.... 900
Albert H. Currier... 1,000
George Howland.. 1,000
Alexander Coignard, two hours a day........................... 400
S. Grace Thompson... 500

DEARBORN SCHOOL,

Madison street, between State and Dearborn.

George D. Broomell, Principal................................$1,000
Anna E. Whittier.. 400
Alice L. Barnard.. 400
Fannie Nicol.. 500
M. Amanda Ramsdell.. 350
Julia M. Sawyer... 325

JONES SCHOOL,

Corner of Clark and Harrison Streets.

Willard Woodward.... ....$1,000
Carrie J. McArthur.. 400
Lavinia C. Perkins.. 400
Margaret Shields.. 500
Claudene C. Packard... 325
Marion A. Grennell.. 325
Mary E. Hall.... 275

SCAMMON SCHOOL,

Madison Street, between Halstead and Union.

Daniel S. Wentworth, Principal..............................$1,500
Helen Culver.. 400
Mary L. Reed.. 400
Adelia Wadsworth.. 500
Charlotte C. Nisbett.. 350
Caroline E. Bickford.. 350
Helen P. Young... 350

BRANCH OF SCAMMON SCHOOL,

Jefferson Street Church, between Washington and Madison.

Susan A. Culver...$425
Jennie E. McLaren.. 275

KINZIE SCHOOL,

Corner of Ohio and La Salle Streets.

Philip Atkinson, Principal.......................................$1,000
Elsie H. Gould... 350
Nette Perry... 300
Cynthia J. Barnes... 500
Kate M. Sullivan.. 250
Bridget A. Kelly.. 250

FRANKLIN SCHOOL,

Corner of Division and Sedgwick Streets.

William Drake, Principal...$1,000
Marion B. Sinclair.. 400
Emma Dickerman... 400
Agnes M. Manning... 500
Naomi Dougall.. 325
Emilia Stoops.. 250
Martha J. Larson... 250

BRANCH OF FRANKLIN SCHOOL,

Larrabee Street.

Emma Hooke..$350

WASHINGTON SCHOOL,

Corner of Owen and Sangamon Streets.

George A. Low, Principal,..$1,000
Fannie H. Smith,.. 400
Annie Kennicott,... 400
Amanda S. Duncan,... 500
Mary C. Wadsworth,.. 350
Kate K. Raworth,... 350

MOSELEY SCHOOL,

Corner of Michigan Avenue and Monterey Streets.

Bradford Y. Averill, Principal,..................................$1,000
Mary E. Doble,... 325
Catharine C. Fox,.. 450
Phebe J. Chapman,... 325

Lucinda E. Dutton,... 250
Sarah S. Hunt,.. 250
Rachel A. Coale,.. 250

BROWN SCHOOL,

Corner of Warren and Page Streets.

Henry M. Keith, Principal,.....................................$1,000
Harriet M. Wentworth,.. 250
Sophia L. Dean,.. 250
Julia E. W. Keith,... 450
Allie Loveless,.. 325
M. Frances Wentworth,.. 250

FOSTER SCHOOL,

Union Street, near Twelfth.

George W. Spofford, Principal,................................. $900
Sarah Mahoney,... 300
Lucy E. Ransom,.. 300
Susan E. Ransom,... 325
Sarah K. Foster,... 350
Sophia A. Dow,... 250
M. Louise Wilson,.. 300
Emeline S. Haley,.. 250
Sarah E. Bliss,.. 250
Elizabeth J. Cory,... 250
Hattie A. Strong,.. 250

OGDEN SCHOOL,

Chestnut Street, between Dearborn and Wolcott.

Appleton H. Fitch, Principal,.................................$1,000
Elizabeth H. Bennett,.. 300
Ann M. Shattuck,... 325
Fannie Brown,.. 400
Lucy A. Wright,.. 250
Mary E. Reed,.. 250
Sarah E. Austin,... 250

TEACHER OF MUSIC,

William Tillinghast,...$1,000

BOUNDARIES OF DISTRICTS.

Dearborn School. — That portion of the South Division situated between the main branch of the Chicago river and Jackson street.

Jones School. — That portion of the South Division situated between Jackson street and Twelfth street.

Scammon School. — That portion of West Chicago bounded on the north by Randolph street, on the east by the South Branch of the Chicago river, on the south by Tyler street and a line due east from the centre of Tyler street to the South Branch of the Chicago river, and on the west by Curtiss and Aberdeen streets.

Kinzie School. — That portion of the North Division of the city bounded on the north by Chicago avenue from the North Branch of the Chicago river to Wells street, thence on the east by Wells street to Huron street, thence on the north by Huron street to Clark street, thence on the east by Clark street to the Main Branch of the Chicago river, on the south by the Main Branch of the Chicago river, and on the west by the North Branch of the Chicago river.

Franklin School. — That portion of the North Division of the city bounded on the north by the city limits, from the North Branch of the Chicago river to Lake Michigan, thence on the east by Lake Michigan to North Avenue, thence on the south by North Avenue to Clark street, thence on the east by Clark street to Oak street, thence on the south by Oak street to Wells street, thence on the east by Wells street to Chicago Avenue, thence on the south by Chicago Avenue to the North Branch of the Chicago river.

Washington School. — That portion of the West Division bounded on the north by the city limits and the North Branch of the Chicago river, on the east by the North Branch of the Chicago river, on the south by Randolph street to Sheldon street, thence on the west by Sheldon street to Kinzie street, thence on the south by Kinzie street to Reuben street thence on the west by Reuben street to Chicago Avenue, thence on the south by Chicago Avenue to the city limits, and on the west by the city limits.

Moseley School. — That portion of the South Division situated south of Twelfth street.

Brown School. — That portion of the West Division of the city bounded on the north by Chicago Avenue, from the city limits to Reuben street, thence on the east by Reuben street to Kinzie street, thence on the north by Kinzie street to Sheldon street, thence on the east by Sheldon street to Randolph street, thence on the north by Randolph street to Curtiss street, thence on the east by Curtiss and Aberdeen streets to Tyler street, thence on the south by Tyler street to Loomis street, thence on the east by Loomis street to Twelfth street, thence on the south by Twelfth street to the city limits, and on the west by the city limits.

5

Foster School. —That portion of the West Division of the city bounded on the north by Twelfth street from the city limits to Loomis street, thence on the west by Loomis street to Tyler street, thence on the north by Tyler street and a line due east from the centre of Tyler street to the South Branch of the Chicago river, on the east and south by the South Branch of the Chicago river, and on the west by the city limits from the South Branch of the Chicago river to Twelfth street.

Ogden School. —That portion of the North Division of the city bounded on the north by North Avenue from Clark street to Lake Michigan, on the east by Lake Michigan, on the south by the Main Branch of the Chicago river, on the west by Clark street from the Main Branch of the Chicago river to Huron street, thence on the south by Huron street to Wells street, thence on the west by Wells street to Oak street, thence on the north by Oak street to Clark street, and thence on the west by Clark street to North Avenue.